1000 WORDS AND PICTURES

compiled by RICHARD POWELL
illustrated by TONY KENYON

Ladybird Books

All about me

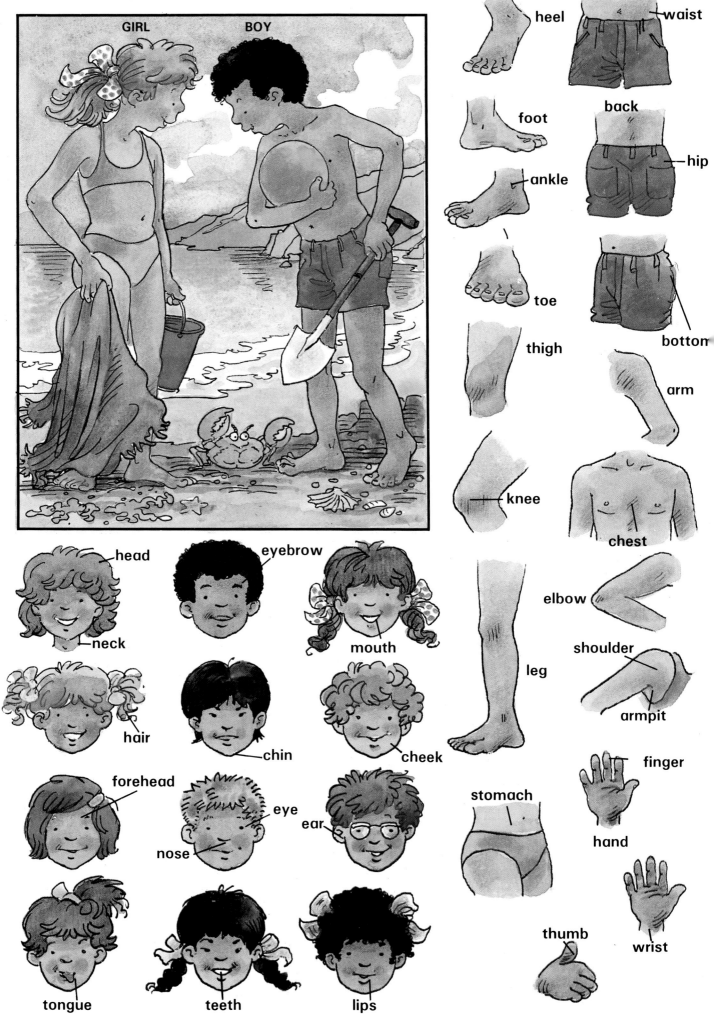

GIRL   BOY

heel
waist
foot
back
ankle
hip
toe
bottom
thigh
arm
knee
chest
head
eyebrow
elbow
neck
mouth
shoulder
leg
hair
chin
cheek
armpit
forehead
eye
finger
nose
ear
stomach
hand
thumb
wrist
tongue
teeth
lips

Clothes

sweater

shorts

cardigan

nightdress

shirt

anorak

pants

skirt

pyjamas

tie

vest

tights

scarf

gloves

trousers

T-shirt

handkerchief

socks

dress

blouse

jumper

rainhat

raincoat

jacket

boots

shoes

3

Families

husband/father/dad

wife/mother/mum

grandad

granny

brother/son

sister/daughter

baby

Pets

kennel

dog

kitten

parrot

guinea pig

tortoise

stable

horse

canary

cage

4

grandma

grandpa

aunt

uncle

twins/cousins

rabbit

hutch

puppy

fish

tank

cat

budgerigar

perch

wheel

mouse

frog

5

Homes

bungalow

hut

caravan

tents

cottage

houseboat

The garden

broom

flowers

snail

bee

apples

fork

basket

worm

ladder

dog

cat

hosepipe

6

chalet

terraced houses

igloo

block of flats

house

ade

trowel

rake

dustbin

tree

wheelbarrow

lawn mower

watering can

window box

grass

7

The kitchen

tin opener

apron

mop

frying pan

cup

saucer

dog bowl

sink

washing-up liquid

draining board

taps

tea towel

stool

plate

mug

brush

dustpan

iron

cupboard

whisk

washing powder

oven

tray

wooden spoon

pedal bin

kettle

washing machine

sieve

rolling pin

tiles

saucepan

freezer

hob

mixing bowl

ironing board

drawer

refrigerator

9

The living room

speaker

table

records

vase

hi-fi

radiator

cushion

magazine

rug

clock

picture

armchair

tape

telephone

bookcase

settee

books

lamp

radio

newspaper

television

The dining room

jug

butter dish

spoon

glass

sideboard

tablecloth

salt

pepper

dining chair

curtains

fruit bowl

fork

knife

table mat

bread board

carpet

plant

sauce bottle

plate

wool

door

The bedroom

alarm clock

slippers

quilt

toy box

teddy bear

desk

curtains

poster

The bathroom

bubbles

shampoo

towel

mirror

scales

shaver

toilet

toilet paper

basin

bath mat

12

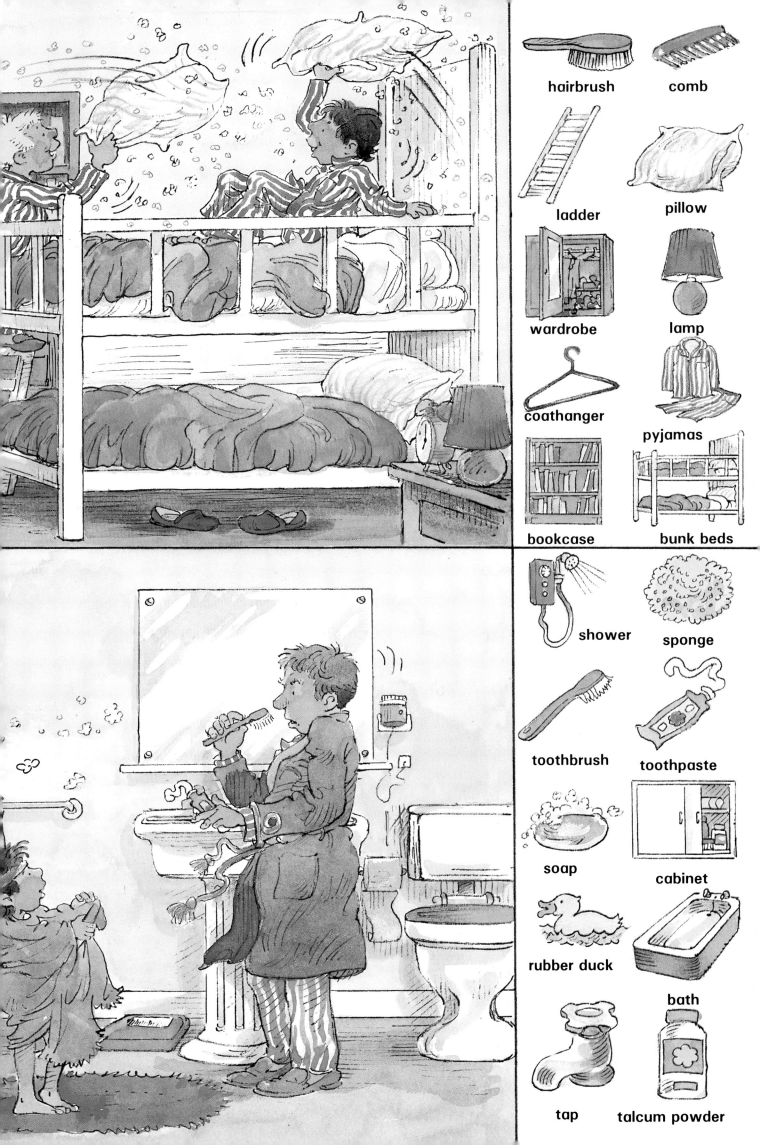

hairbrush

comb

ladder

pillow

wardrobe

lamp

coathanger

pyjamas

bookcase

bunk beds

shower

sponge

toothbrush

toothpaste

soap

cabinet

rubber duck

bath

tap

talcum powder

The street

workman

drain

traffic light

aerial

litter bin

shopping ba

florist shop

lorry

policeman

drill

clock

ice cream van

garage

bicycle

church

bus

bird

baker's shop

van

lamp post

delivery man

pavement

motorcycle

buggy

manhole

driver

car

umbrella

taxi

petrol pump

digger

newsstand

bunch of flowers

water pipe

traffic cone

flats

15

The supermarket

carrots

marrow

cabbage

celery

meat

chicken

cheese

cereal

tins

flour

detergent

yogurt

eggs

trolley

milk

jam

basket

toilet rolls

till

bread

fish

beans **tomatoes** **cucumbers** **sweet corn** **lettuce** **potatoes** **melons**

onions

mushrooms

oranges

pears

apples

lemons

grapes

pineapple

bananas

butter

margarine

  **sugar** **biscuits**  **cashier** **juice** **cream** **customer**

sausages

In hospital

plaster cast

medicine

bandage

get well card

watch

trolley

stethoscope

syringe

nurse

height chart

sling

operating theatre

doctor

plant

television

wheelchair

crutch

thermometer

chart

At the dentist

toothpaste

toothbrush

mouth wash

locker

screen

dentist's chair

false teeth

drill

slippers

bed

dentist

instruments

mask

19

The classroom

paper

clock

map

satchel

chalk

ruler

pens

glue

pencils

compass

calendar

bin

scissors

blackboard

books

crayons

desk

paints

exercise book

rubber

brush

jigsaw

drawing pins

teacher

globe

fish tank

nature chart

scales

computer

21

The park

lead

bone

roller skates

railings

picnic

bench

duck

ribbon

walking stick

flowers

paddling pool

ducklings

slide

cap

swimming costume

litter bin

bber ring

kite

balloon

drinking
fountain

swings

bandstand

wspaper

seesaw

grass

skipping rope

flask

roundabout

jogger

pushchair

bicycle

yacht

23

Wild animals and birds

eagle

raccoon

koala

giraffe

beaver

ostrich

panda

gorilla

zebra

Jeopard

crocodile

flamingo

dolphin

polar bear

hippopotamus

parrot

kangaroo

rhinoceros

lion

cubs

monkey

elephant

camel

pelican

penguin

snake

tiger

seal

walrus

bear

25

The railway station

mailbag

carriage

coal wagon

guard

signal

ticket office

diesel engine

passengers

buffet car

timetable

rucksack

suitcase

cab

buffers

goods train

driver

guard's van

track

luggage trolley

flowers

platform

trolley

vending machine

litter bin

27

The harbour

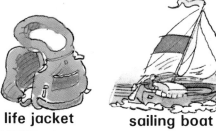

life jacket

sailing boat

quay

cargo ship

porthole

lighthouse

seagull

rope

buoy

tanker

lobster pot

crane

28

funnel

mast

fishing net

tug

lifebuoy

anchor

rowing boat

oar

fishing boat

fish

car ferry

flag

scales

fisherman

29

The airport

control tower

steps

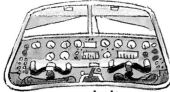
cockpit

runway

fuel tanker

rotor blades

pilot

helicopter

tail

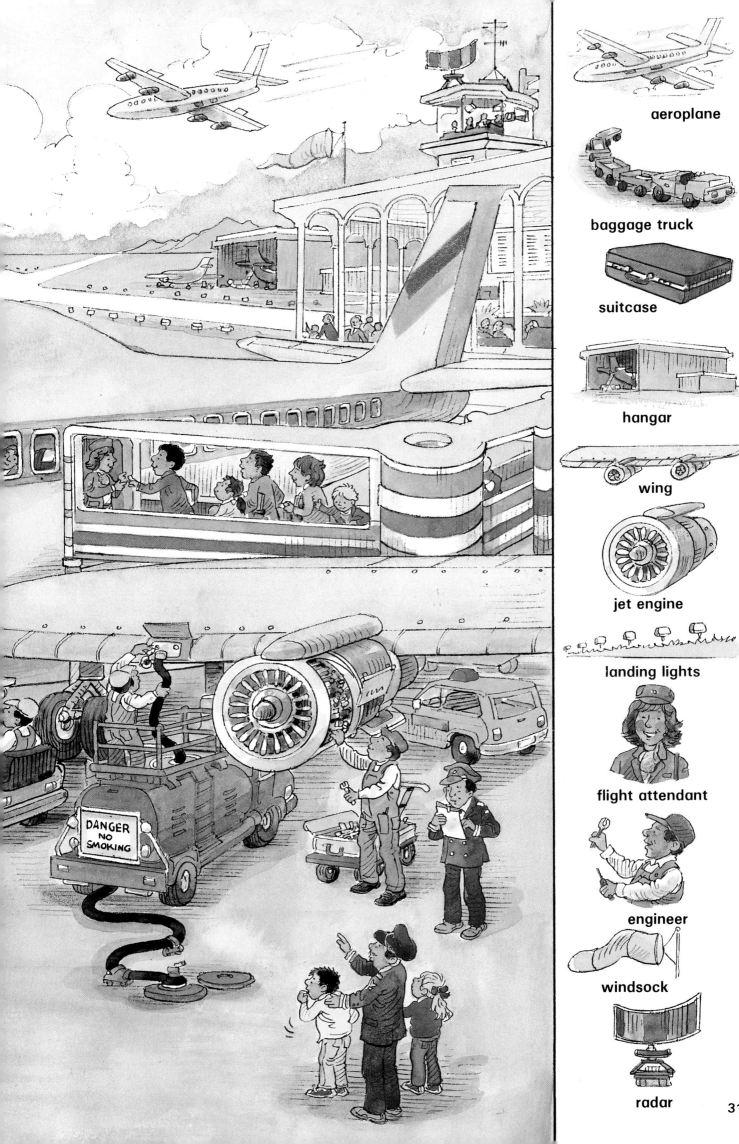

aeroplane

baggage truck

suitcase

hangar

wing

jet engine

landing lights

flight attendant

engineer

windsock

radar

DANGER
NO
SMOKING

31

The bus station

bus

kiosk

timetable

barrier

queue

bus stop

ticket machine

32

busker

conductor

flat tyre

snack bar

postcards

parcel

briefcase

shopping bag

driver

33

The building site

drill

wheelbarrow

crane

bulldozer

electrician

shovel

saw

bricks

plumber

ladder

34

trowel

ricklayer

dumper truck

nails

hammer

welder

pick

hard hat

cement

roof tiles

cement mixer

carpenter

scaffolding

35

The garage

spanner

petrol pump

exhaust pipe

pliers

wing mir...

bonnet

boot

seat belt

engine

windscreen

jack

cool box

tyre

steering wheel

bumper

headlight

mechanic

car wash

air pump

fire extinguisher

oil can

litter bin

On the farm

goose   sheep   lambs   scarecrow   bull

corn

henhouse

plough

baler

combine harvester

farmer

milk tanker

chicks

saddle

field   stable   silo   tractor

horse

cow

pig

turkey

cockerel

hen

duck

ducklings

sheepdog

straw bales

sack

barn

pond

farmhouse

trailer

hay

gate

pigsty

broom

cart

sickle

cowshed

39

The countryside

leaf

tree

lake

bee

kit

fly

dragonfly

footpath

hiker

ladybird

beetle

rucksack

butterfly

rowing boat

village

field

bridge

river

angler

caravan

squirrel

signpost

fish

otter

fishing rod

nest

rabbit

frog

mountain

waterfall

bush

caterpillar

bird

log

mallet

deer

map

skier

cable car

tent

barbecue

At the seaside

sun hat

air bed

deck chair

swimmer

beach ball

ice cream

windbreak

pebbles

sun

snorkel

flippers

starfish

suntan lotion

rubber ring

trunks

spade

bucket

swimming costume

sailing boat

lighthouse

radio

surfer

net

bikini

buoy

seagull

cave

seashell

rock

wave

telescope

crab

rockpool

sunglasses

sandcastle

sailboard

speedboat

beach

seaweed

dinghy

43

Weather words

clouds   flood   wind

**MONTHS
OF THE
YEAR**

January

February

March

April

May

June

July

August

September

October

November

December

WINDY

STORMY

dew

fog

snowman

frost

rainbow

mist

gale

snowball

SUNNY

sun

snow

thunder and lightning

whirlwind

SNOWY

puddle

breeze

ice

rain

storm

45

Things we do

catch

throw

sneeze

jump

drink

ski

skip

swim

eat

sing

sleep

wave

clap

push

write

run

laugh

paint

sit

stand

climb

read

pull

trip

buy

cry

wash

walk

sew

dry

play

dig

dance

watch

listen

cut

dress

yawn

sweep

frown

lick

stick

People

mountaineer

artist

butcher

American footballer

dustman

weight-lifter

typist

decorator

athlete

dentist

taxi driver

carpenter

chef

tennis player

diver

astronaut

skier

hairdresser

jockey

postman

skater

miner

waiter

firefighter

optician

scientist

singer

doctor

baker

lumberjack

policeman

gymnast

computer programmer

Opposite words

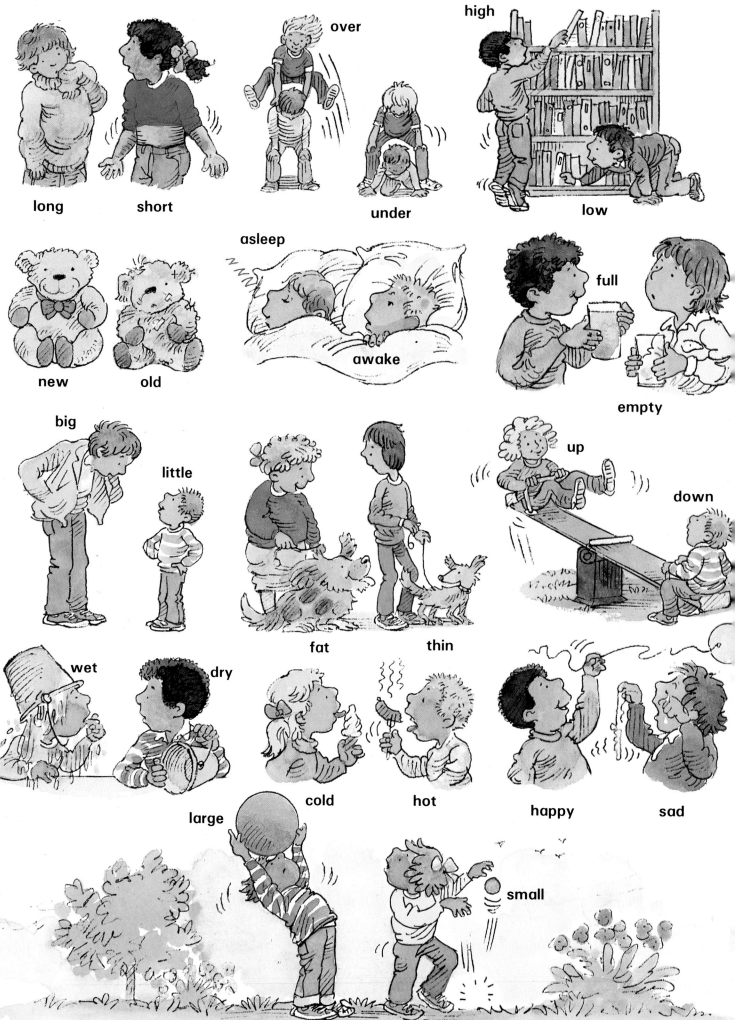

long   short

over

under

high

low

asleep

awake

new   old

full

empty

big

little

fat   thin

up

down

wet   dry

cold   hot

happy   sad

large

small

My week

Monday

I bought a toy plane.

Tuesday

I went to my friend's house to fly my plane.

Wednesday

After school, I flew my plane again. It flew well.

Thursday

I went to Grandma's house. My plane came down with a crash.

Friday

I couldn't fly my plane.

Saturday

Today Mum mended my plane.

Sunday

My plane crashed again. I think I'll buy a bigger, stronger one next week... or perhaps a rocket.

What time is it?

half past nine

The bus is coming!

quarter to three

Let's go to the park

half past four

Home time

half past seven

Time for a story and goodnight!

eight o'clock

Time to sit down!

Colours and shapes

Find these colours in the picture...

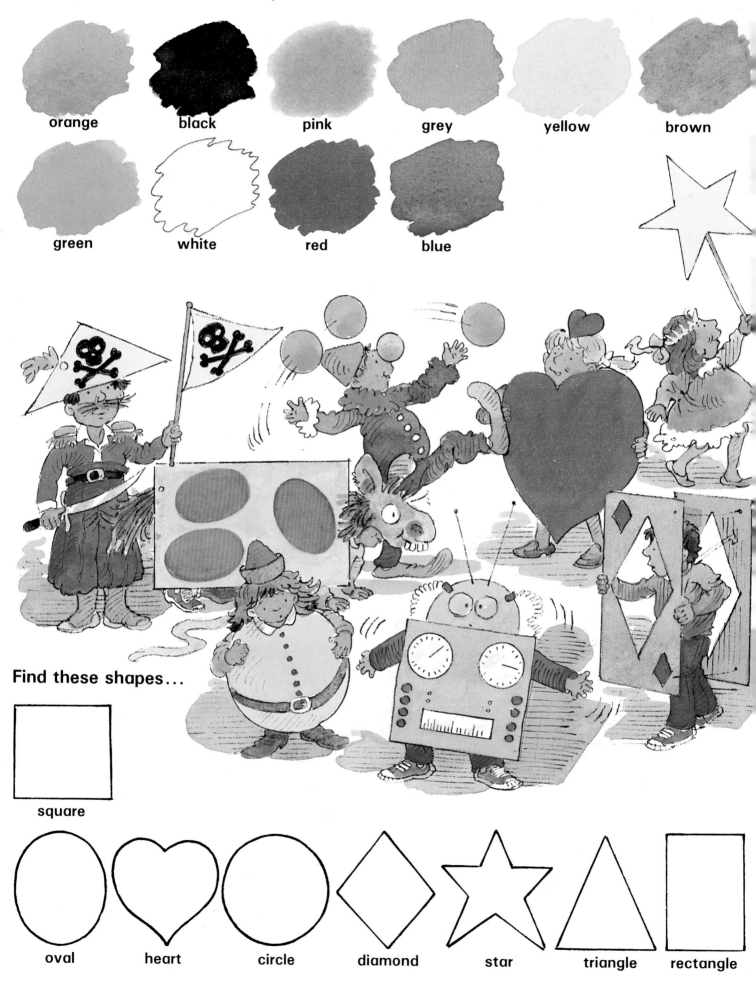

orange

black

pink

grey

yellow

brown

green

white

red

blue

Find these shapes...

square

oval

heart

circle

diamond

star

triangle

rectangle

Numbers

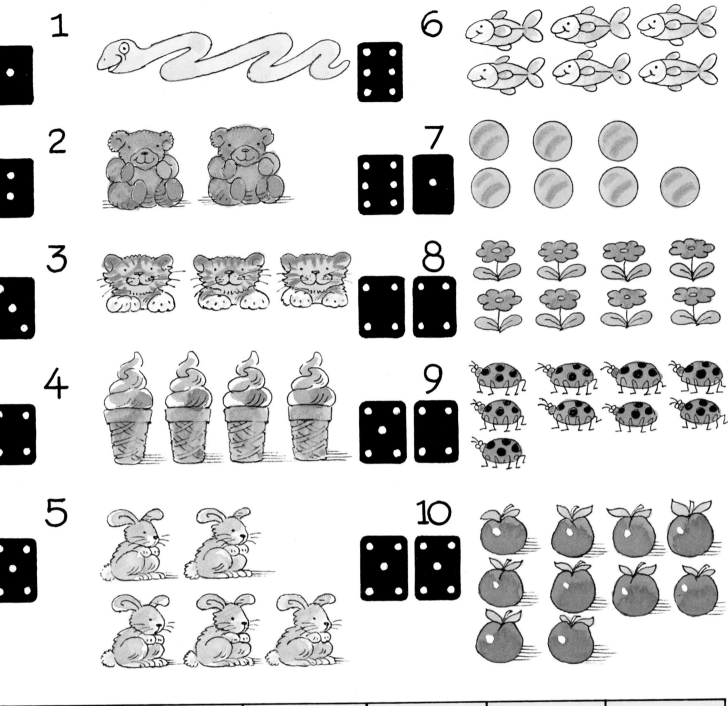

1 one	6 six	11 eleven	16 sixteen	30 thirty	80 eighty
2 two	7 seven	12 twelve	17 seventeen	40 forty	90 ninety
3 three	8 eight	13 thirteen	18 eighteen	50 fifty	100 one hundred
4 four	9 nine	14 fourteen	19 nineteen	60 sixty	1,000 one thousand
5 five	10 ten	15 fifteen	20 twenty	70 seventy	1,000,000 one million

Index

A

action words 46-47
aerial 14
aeroplane 31
air bed 42
airport 30-31
air pump 37
alarm clock 12
American footballer 48
anchor 29
angler 40
animals 24-25
ankle 2
anorak 3
apples 6, 17
April 44
apron 8
arm 2
armchair 10
armpit 2
artist 48
asleep 50
astronaut 49
athlete 48
August 44
aunt 5
awake 50

B

baby 4
back 2
baggage truck 31
baker 49
baker's shop 15
baler 38
bales 39
balloon 23
bananas 17
bandage 18
bandstand 23
barbecue 41
barn 39
barrier 32
basin 12
basket 6, 16
bath 13, 52
bath mat 12
bathroom 12-13
beach 43
beach ball 42

beans 17
bear 12, 24, 25
beaver 24
bed 19
bedroom 12-13
bee 6, 40
beetle 40
bench 22
bicycle 15, 23
big 50
bikini 43
bin 20, 22
bird 15, 41
birds 24-25
biscuits 17
black 54
blackboard 21
block of flats 7, 15
blouse 3
blue 54
boat 28, 29, 42
body words 2
bone 22
bonnet 36
bookcase 10, 13
books 10, 21
boot 36
boots 3
bottom 2
bowl 8, 9
boy 2
bread 16
bread board 11
breakfast 52
breeze 45
bricklayer 35
bricks 34
bridge 40
briefcase 33
broom 6, 39
brother 4
brown 54
brush 8
brush (paint) 21
bubbles 12
bucket 42
budgerigar 5
buffers 27
buffet car 26
buggy 15
building site 34-35
bull 38
bulldozer 34
bumper 37
bunch of flowers 15
bungalow 6

bunk beds 13
buoy 28, 43
bus 15, 32, 53
bus station 32-33
bus stop 32
bush 41
busker 33
butcher 48
butter 17
butter dish 11
butterfly 40
buy 47

C

cab 27
cabbage 16
cabinet 13
cable car 41
cage 4
calendar 20
camel 25
canary 4
cap 22
car 15
caravan 7, 41
card 18
cardigan 3
car ferry 29
cargo ship 28
carpenter 35, 48
carpet 11
carriage 26
carrots 16
cart 39
car wash 37
cashier 17
cat 5, 6
catch 46
caterpillar 41
cave 43
celery 16
cement 35
cement mixer 35
cereal 16
chair 10, 11
chalet 7
chalk 20
chart 18, 19, 21
cheek 2
cheese 16
chef 48
chest 2
chicken 16

chicks 38
chin 2
church 15
circle 54
clap 46
classroom 20-21
climb 46
clock 10, 14, 20
clothes 3
clouds 44
coal wagon 26
coathanger 13
cockerel 39
cockpit 30
cold 50
colours 54
comb 13
combine harvester 38
compass 20
computer 21
computer programmer 49
conductor 33
cone 15
control tower 30
corn 38
cottage 6
countryside 40-41
cousins 5
cow 39
cowshed 39
crab 43
crane 28, 34
crash 51
crayons 21
cream 17
crocodile 24
crutch 18
cry 47
cubs 25
cucumbers 17
cup 8
cupboard 9
curtains 11, 12
cushion 10
customer 17
cut 47

D

dad 4
dance 47
daughter 4
days 51
December 44
deck chair 42
decorator 48

deer 41
delivery man 15
dentist 19, 48
dentist's chair 19
desk 12, 21
detergent 16
dew 44
diamond 54
diesel engine 26
dig 47
digger 15
dinghy 43
dining chair 11
dining room 11
diver 48
doctor 18, 49
dog 4, 6, 39
dog bowl 8
dolphin 24
door 11
down 50
dragonfly 40
drain 14
draining board 8
drawer 9
drawing pins 21
dress 3, 47
drill 14, 19, 34
drink 46
drinking fountain 23
driver 15, 27, 33, 48
dry 47, 50
duck 13, 22, 39
ducklings 22, 39
dumper truck 35
dustbin 7
dustman 48
dustpan 8

E

eagle 24
ear 2
eat 46
eggs 16
eight 55
eighteen 55
eighty 55
elbow 2
electrician 34
elephant 25
eleven 55
empty 50
engine 26, 36

engineer 31
exercise book 21
exhaust pipe 36
eye 2
eyebrow 2

F

false teeth 19
families 4-5
farm 38-39
farmer 38
farmhouse 39
fat 50
father 4
February 44
ferry 29
field 38, 40
fifteen 55
fifty 55
finger 2
fire extinguisher 37
firefighter 49
fish 5, 16, 29, 41
fisherman 29
fishing boat 29
fishing net 29
fishing rod 41
fish tank 21
five 55
flag 29
flamingo 24
flask 23
flat tyre 33
flats 7, 15
flight attendant 31
flippers 42
flood 44
florist shop 14
flour 16
flowers 6, 15, 22, 27
fly 40, 51
fog 44
foot 2
footpath 40
forehead 2
fork 6, 11
forty 55
fountain 23
four 55
fourteen 55
freezer 9
Friday 51
frog 5, 41

frost 45
frown 47
fruit bowl 11
frying pan 8
fuel tanker 30
full 50
funnel 29

G

gale 45
garage 15, 36-37
garden 6-7
gate 39
get well card 18
giraffe 24
girl 2
glass 11
globe 21
gloves 3
glue 20
goods train 27
goose 38
gorilla 24
grandad 4
grandma 5, 51
grandpa 5
granny 4
grapes 17
grass 7, 23
green 54
grey 54
guard 26
guard's van 27
guinea pig 4
gymnast 49

H

hair 2
hairbrush 13
hairdresser 49
half past 53
hammer 35
hand 2
handkerchief 3
hangar 31
happy 50
harbour 28-29
hard hat 35
hay 39
head 2

headlight 37
heart 54
heel 2
height chart 18
helicopter 30
hen 39
henhouse 38
hi-fi 10
high 50
hiker 40
hip 2
hippopotamus 24
hob 9
homes 6-7
horse 4, 39
hosepipe 6
hospital 18-19
hot 50
house 7, 51
houseboat 6
hundred 55
hungry 52
husband 4
hut 6
hutch 5

I

ice 45
ice cream 42
ice cream van 14
igloo 7
instruments 19
iron 9
ironing board 9

J

jack 36
jacket 3
jam 16
January 44
jet engine 31
jigsaw 21
jockey 49
jogger 23
jug 11
juice 17
July 44
jump 46
jumper 3
June 44

K

kangaroo 25
kennel 4
kettle 9
kiosk 32
kitchen 8-9
kite 23, 40
kitten 4
knee 2
knife 11
koala 24

L

ladder 6, 13, 34
ladybird 40
lake 40
lambs 38
lamp 10, 13
lamp post 15
landing lights 31
large 50
laugh 46
lawn mower 7
lead 22
leaf 40
leg 2
lemons 17
leopard 24
lettuce 17
lick 47
lifebuoy 29
life jacket 28
light 14
lighthouse 28, 42
lightning 45
lion 25
lips 2
listen 47
litter bin 14, 22, 27, 37
little 50
living room 10
lobster 28
lobster pot 28
locker 19
log 41
long 50
lorry 14
low 50
luggage trolley 27
lumberjack 49
lunch 52

M

magazine 10
mailbag 26
mallet 41
manhole 15
map 20, 41
March 44
margarine 17
marrow 16
mask 19
mast 29
May 44
me 2
meat 16
mechanic 37
medicine 18
melons 17
milk 16
milk tanker 38
million 55
miner 49
mirror 12, 36
mist 45
mixing bowl 9
Monday 51
monkey 25
months 44
mop 8
mother 4
motorcycle 15
mountaineer 48
mountain 41
mouse 5
mouth 2
mouth wash 19
mug 8
mum 4, 51
mushrooms 17

N

nails 35
nature chart 21
neck 2
nest 41
net 43
new 50
newspaper 10, 23
newsstand 15
nightdress 3
nine 55
nineteen 55

ninety 55
nose 2
November 44
numbers 55
nurse 18

O

oar 29
o'clock 52, 53
October 44
oil can 37
old 50
one 55
onions 17
operating theatre 18
opposite words 50
optician 49
orange 54
oranges 17
ostrich 24
otter 41
oval 54
oven 9
over 50

P

paddling pool 22
paint 46
paints 21
panda 24
pants 3
paper 20
parcel 33
park 22-23, 53
parrot 4, 25
passengers 26
pavement 15
pears 17
pebbles 42
pedal bin 9
pelican 25
pencils 20
penguin 25
pens 20
people 48-49
pepper 11
perch 5
petrol pump 15, 36
pets 4-5
pick 35
picnic 22

picture 10
pig 39
pigsty 39
pillow 13
pilot 30
pineapple 17
pink 54
plane 51
plant 11, 18
plaster cast 18
plate 8, 11
platform 27
play 47
pliers 36
plough 38
plumber 34
polar bear 24
policeman 14, 49
pond 39
porthole 28
postcards 33
poster 12
postman 49
potatoes 17
puddle 45
pull 46
puppy 5
push 46
pushchair 23
pyjamas 3, 13

Q

quarter past 52
quarter to 52, 53
quay 28
queue 32
quilt 12

R

rabbit 5, 41
raccoon 24
radar 31
radiator 10
radio 10, 43
railings 22
railway station 26-27
rain 45
rainbow 45
raincoat 3
rainhat 3
rake 7